MW00907591

Penelope the Peacock

Copyright 2018
Story by Paris Goodyear-Brown LCSW, RPT-S
Illustrations by Eric Gott LPC-MHSP
Formatted by Jessica Hargrove

This book is the answer to a question asked by a 9 year old Nepalese boy who was was conceived during the time his mother was being trafficked. Recently, I was providing training on trauma-informed care to a group of houseparents in Kathmandu, Nepal. These houseparents care for children and teens who had been sold into the sex trade in India, eventually rescued, and brought back to Nepal to live. After listening to the first day of training, one of the training organizers came to me and asked me what she should say to a mother in her care. This mother had been sold into slavery as a teenager and ended up in a brothel in India. During her enslavement, she became pregnant by one of the men who raped her. She gave birth to a son and during the period of time that she was forced to be a sex worker, hid him under the bed. Eventually the mother and son were rescued and came to live in a safe place. They lived in a home with other rescued girls for several years, surrounded mainly by mamas and aunties. Eventually the son went to school and began to hear about fathers and daddies from his classmates. One day, he came home from school and asked his mother this question: "Who is my daddy?" Mom was overwhelmed with the complexity of the question and the potential that she might harm him with her answer. She excused herself, went into the bathroom and cried for herself and for her son. When she returned from the bathroom, her son's attention had been distracted by something else. He has continued to ask about his daddy periodically, and to ask if the color of his skin, which is different than mom's, comes from his father. She remains at a loss for what to say to her son. When asked by this training organizer, "What should I tell this mother to tell her son?" the question became one I needed to try to answer.

Human trafficking is unconscionable. A young girl becoming pregnant as a result of rape is equally unconscionable. But for me, the most unconscionable act is to leave this child without an answer to his question. Most of us wrestle to find the words to answer these hard, hard questions…but we must try. This is my attempt. My hope is that his preciousness is amplified through the story as the hard truths of his beginnings are held in age appropriate ways.

Penelope was a very special peacock. She was born with the remarkable feathers that are usually reserved just for the males of the species.

She was the firstborn among many brothers and sisters and should have held a place of honor, but she lived on a large peacock farm and there were many hardships.

There was barely enough grain to go around and it took lots of time to gather it. When she was little, Penelope went with her parents to gather the grain. They would go out early in the morning and press against the other peacocks all day long. As she got older she would sometimes babysit her younger brothers and sisters and sometimes she was made to go out alone to get the grain.

Either way Penelope was almost always working. She never got to play pick-up sticks with the other peacocks and she only got to go to school now and then.

Then one night, after a long day's pecking, she returned home carrying a large basket of grain on her back. She set it down by the front door, relieved to have the weight removed. She turned around and noticed that her parent peacocks were sitting with a large male bird that she had never seen before. He smiled when he saw her...and it was not a nice smile.

"Aah," he said in satisfaction,

"She has very many pretty feathers."

His accent when he spoke sounded clipped and harsh. Her eyes tracked to her father's hands. In them was a suitcase, and in the suitcase were her few prized possessions. She watched her father give the suitcase to this stranger and he told her she must go with this stranger right now.

Penelope asked why and her heart started to race when her parent peacocks looked away. Papa peacock said,
"This will help us to get more grain."
Penelope did as she was told and went with the stranger.

After hours of bumping along dusty roads they arrived at another farm, but it wasn't just for peacocks. There were many other species of bird...she had never seen so many beautiful birds in one place. The stranger said,

"Welcome to the Feather Farm."

He ushered her into a room and said,

"Stay here."

Penelope waited, alone, scared, and confused. When the stranger returned he had an animal with him. She had never seen other animals, only peacocks and the farmer, so she didn't know how to distinguish a cow's tail from a pig's tail, but was forced to learn these differences quickly.

The first animal came in,
looked her over top to bottom
and then said,
"Alright. I'll take one."
Before she could even wonder
what he was taking he came
over and yanked out one of her
tail feathers.

Penelope gasped from the sting of it and wasn't sure which was more painful...the way her body ached as it was pulled out or the sure and sudden knowledge that the feather was gone forever. There was no way to grow a new one. The animal stopped at the door, handed the stranger some grain and left. The stranger dropped a few kernels of grain on the floor for her and without even turning to look at her, walked out.

Penelope tried to care for her hurt place and spent time re-arranging her feathers to try to cover the hole. Just when she had started to convince herself that no one would notice the missing tailfeather, the door swung wide again.

A different animal was there and as he quietly closed the door behind him, she began to understand that the taking had only begun.

One by one her tailfeathers were stolen from her. Sometimes they were plucked violently. The plucking hurt so much she wanted to cry. She did cry at first until...but crying was work and she needed all her energy to survive the animals. Other times the animals were kind of nice, even shy, about asking for a feather. But in the end, they all took one.

After awhile, Penelope stopped trying to hide the holes. She stopped eating even the meager grain she was given. She avoided the mirror, as she was ashamed at what she saw. She felt dirty from all the paws and claws and beaks and talons that touched her as they chose their feather. One day ran into the next and the only time of day she wished for was the time that she could sleep.

Then one day she woke up and felt a little different. She had a small pang in her tummy and although she had almost forgotten what hunger felt like, she realized she was hungry.

In fact, she was hungrier than she had been in a long, long time. She ate what she could and asked for more.

She began to gain weight and her remaining feathers seems to have a new sheen to them.

The seasons were changing and every morning the sun shone briefly into her bedroom window, waking her. Most mornings she rolled right over and went back to sleep, but on this particular morning she couldn't quite get comfortable...it was like she was sleeping on a stone. She went to rearrange her straw and there it was...an egg.

Could it be? Her very own egg? Her very own baby?
Somewhere, in the midst of all the taking done
by the animals, one had left something precious...new life.

Instantly, Penelope's focus shifted from simply
surviving the animals to protecting her little one.
She had hope for the first time since she came to
the feather farm and a fierce determination that
she would not stay. She ate and drank and warmed
her egg. When the animals came to take
feathers she was comforted by the
knowledge that she was no longer alone.
Each day, when the animals left she
worked on her nest, a place to snuggle
with her baby.

The day that her baby hatched, she gasped with delight when she saw him...for not only was he healthy and strong, but he was the most surprising and magnificent shade of white she had ever seen. In fact, he only had white feathers. She wondered if one of the albino animals had left some of his talon when taking a feather, as she did not think the shiny whiteness was from her alone.

As Penelope gazed upon her perfectly formed and stunningly pure white baby, she felt a fierce determination rise up in her. She must escape. She could not bear the idea of any animal taking even one feather from her baby. She began then to create a plan.

She had heard rumblings of other birds who decided to leave and found a way out. She had noticed the disappearance of two separate birds on the same day weeks before. She learned of a network of helpers who rescued birds who had been trapped on feather farms.

Penelope waited patiently, gathering what was needed to go. Whenever an animal came to take a feather, she would focus on the plan to leave, and each time she would hide her baby safely under the nest where the animals couldn't see.

Each night she snuggled him and talked of the new life they would have...and one night, very quietly and with some help, they slipped off of the feather farm forever.

They found others who had been on feather farms and together they made a new kind of family. Penelope and her baby were safe and could start to heal.

She watched her baby grow into a
fine young peacock who was as kind on
the inside as he was handsome on the outside.

One day he asked his mom about where he came from. He wondered about his daddy. She had known this question would come. Penelope explained that she didn't know for sure which creature had helped to make him. She said,

"My time at the feather farm was dark and scary. When I realized that you were growing, I thought...Here he is! The one truly right, bright gift out of all the wrong."

Penelope looked deeply into her son's eyes and said,

"I don't know who your father was, but I do know who you are...and I know who we are together."

And they agreed that this would be enough.

Every day, all over the world, children and teens are sold into slavery and forced to become sex workers or unpaid labor. Every year 300,000 children are taken worldwide, but this problem is not just happening on the other side of the world. It is in our backyards, in our neighborhoods. Trafficking crimes have been confirmed in every one of the 50 United States of America and statistics place the annual number of US children trafficked at somewhere between 25,000 and 33,000 per year. The report issued in 2002 by the International Labor Organization, which estimates that 1.2 million children a year are trafficked, continues to be the most common statistic referenced, although the actual number of victims remains unknowable. Many organizations now exist which work to prevent trafficking by equipping disenfranchised populations with education, infrastructure, vocational training, and sustainable livelihoods.

Many minors who end up in the sex trade have a history of sexual abuse, maltreatment and neglect. These young people sometimes run away from home or act out in such ways that they get put into group homes. Traffickers target these children and teens, often preying on their low self-esteem, making them feel special and offering gifts or false promises to lure them into slavery. Safe grown-ups who know what to look for and how to help when we see it can help in turning the tide for at-risk children. Learn all you can and do what you can.

The National Human Trafficking Hotline is a national 24-hour, toll-free, multilingual anti-trafficking hotline. Call 1-888-373-7888 to report a tip; connect with anti-trafficking services in your area; or request training and technical assistance, general information, or specific anti-trafficking resources. The Hotline is equipped to handle calls from all regions of the United States from a wide range of callers including, but not limited to: potential trafficking victims, community members, law enforcement, medical professionals, legal professionals, service providers, researchers, students, and policymakers.

Proceeds from the sale of this book will be used to fund mental health services for trafficking survivors and to equip their caregivers to provide trauma-informed healing care.